For Luke and Sophie

Henry Holt and Company, LLC, *Publishers since 1866*
175 Fifth Avenue, New York, New York 10010
mackids.com

Henry Holt® is a registered trademark of
Henry Holt and Company, LLC.
Copyright © 2012 by Randy Cecil
All rights reserved.

Library of Congress Cataloging-in-Publication Data
Cecil, Randy.
Horsefly and Honeybee / Randy Cecil. — 1st ed.
p.   cm.
Summary: Honeybee and Horsefly have a fight that results in each of them losing a wing and being forced to
walk, but when they are both captured by hungry Bullfrog their only hope of escape is to work together.
ISBN 978-0-8050-9300-1 (hc)
[1. Cooperativeness—Fiction. 2. Horseflies—Fiction. 3. Flies—Fiction.
4. Honeybee—Fiction. 5. Bees—Fiction. 6. Bullfrog—Fiction.] I. Title.
PZ7.C2999Hor 2012   [E]—dc23   2011029044

First Edition—2012 / Designed by April Ward
The artist used oil paint on paper to create the illustrations for this book.
Printed in China by South China Printing Company Ltd., Dongguan City, Guangdong Province.

3   5   7   9   10   8   6   4

Horsefly
and
Honeybee

RANDY CECIL

Henry Holt and Company
New York

Honeybee was tired.

So she stretched and yawned
and plopped down inside a
flower for a nap.

But Horsefly was
already inside.

They had a fight.

It wasn't pretty.

Horsefly lost a wing.
Honeybee lost a wing, too.

"Drat!" said Horsefly.
Then he ran away.
"Drat!" said Honeybee.
And she ran away, too.

Honeybee started the long walk home.

She walked slowly and took lots of breaks.

Honeybee wasn't used to walking,
but with just one wing she couldn't fly.

Then she came upon a pond.
What could she do?
She couldn't fly over it.

Suddenly, she was
grabbed from behind.

"Drat!" said Honeybee.

Bullfrog licked his lips
as he carried her deep into
the pond.

He plopped Honeybee down on a lily pad—right next to Horsefly! Then Bullfrog went away in search of more dinner.

"Drat!" said Horsefly.
"Drat!" said Honeybee.

They sat there for a long time.
Horsefly pouted.
Honeybee pouted.

Horsefly moaned.
Honeybee moaned.

And then they heard
Bullfrog coming back.

Horsefly grabbed Honeybee.
Honeybee grabbed Horsefly.

They each
flapped a wing—

and up they went!

"Drat!" said Bullfrog.
He hopped faster.

He shot his sticky tongue
into the air after them.
But Horsefly and
Honeybee were already
out of reach.

"Drat!" said Bullfrog.

Together, Honeybee and
Horsefly flew far away.

They flew and flew,
and finally they landed
on a flower.

And there was plenty
of room for them both.

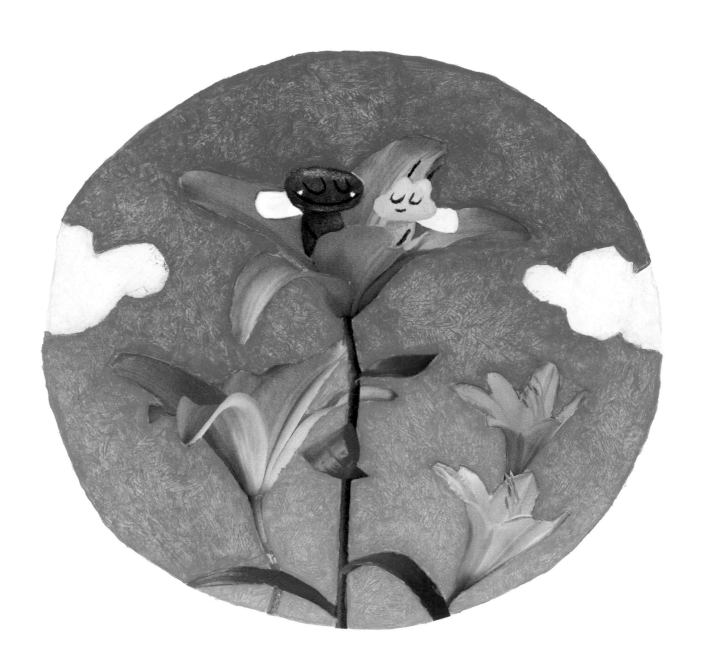

"We are each of us angels with only
one wing, and we can only fly
by embracing one another."

—Luciano De Crescenzo